UNDERWORLDS

The Battle Begins

UNDERWORLDS

BOOK ONE

—

THE BATTLE BEGINS

BY TONY ABBOTT

ILLUSTRATED BY
ANTONIO JAVIER CAPARO

Scholastic Inc.
NEW YORK TORONTO LONDON AUCKLAND
SYDNEY MEXICO CITY NEW DELHI HONG KONG

TO MY FAMILY

ISBN 978-0-545-30831-1

Text copyright © 2011 by Robert T. Abbott

Illustrations copyright © 2011 by Scholastic Inc.

All rights reserved. Published by Scholastic Inc.

SCHOLASTIC and associated logos are trademarks and/or registered trademarks of Scholastic Inc.

12 11 10 9 8 7 6 5 4 3   11 12 13 14 15 16/0

Printed in the U.S.A.   40
First printing, November 2011
DESIGNED BY TIM HALL

CHAPTER ONE

HELP . . .

LOOKING BACK, I TOTALLY SHOULD HAVE EXPECTED the school floor to crack open and flames to spew out all over the place.

There were signs the whole morning that things weren't normal anymore. But it's just not something you imagine happening.

The floor opening up like that.

Smoke suddenly everywhere.

And Dana Runson suddenly nowhere.

I tried to help her, I really did. But she was gone in a flash. Just *gone*. I couldn't believe it.

Not then.

Not until the red wolf and the crazy lunch ladies and the huge guy with horns and the army of metal dudes —

Hold on. I'm telling this backward.

Let me start again.

Before the world flipped upside down and I lost whatever cool I had, this morning started pretty much like any morning.

With my dad's voice.

"Owen Brown, get down here!"

I leaped out of bed, splashed water on my face, and threw on my clothes. Then I raced to the kitchen and flopped down at the table next to my little sister, Mags.

"Sorry," I said. "I couldn't sleep. I was worrying about the concert."

I play guitar in the school orchestra. We were doing a big benefit concert at the local college that morning.

"You'll be great," my mom said. "Eat."

As she slid a bowl of oatmeal in front of me, my dad reached into his wallet. "Take a couple dollars for your collections," he said.

Besides the benefit concert, there are at least four collections going on every day at school. Flood relief. Earthquake relief. Hunger relief. Senior citizen housing. They're all part of our H.E.R.O. program. H.E.R.O. stands for *Help Everyone By Reaching Out.*

Which I know spells H.E.B.R.O. But that's not really a word, so we skip the *B.*

"Me, too," said Mags, pushing a handful of pennies across the table. "I've colored Mr. Lincoln's hair with a blue marker. So everyone will know they're from me."

I slid the coins into my pocket. "Nine cents is perfect, Mags. We'll meet our goal for sure."

"Yay!" she said. "Plus, you know what else? Dana comes home with you today!"

Dana Runson is my oldest friend. Her mother (my mom's college roommate) and father are teachers at the local college. They called last night to ask if Dana could stay here while they went to Iceland to do some research. I know, right? Iceland? *Brrrr!*

Since Dana lives across town, her parents are dropping her off at school this morning, and she'll come home with me and live with us until they get back.

Beep-beep!

"There's the bus," my mom said. "Hustle!"

"See you later! With Dana!" I said. I grabbed my guitar case and tore out of the house to the corner. The bus driver was just beginning to close the door when I leaped on board.

Cool move, right?

Wrong.

The moment I plunked down next to a tall kid listening to his iPod, I realized I had gotten on the high school bus!

Was that the first thing to go weird today?

Luckily, the high school was just across the street from Pinewood Bluffs Elementary. If I ran, I could make it to homeroom before the bell. So I pulled out the dollar bills my dad had given me and carefully folded each of them into airplane shapes.

"You making origami?" asked the boy next to me.

"Just saving time," I said. "There's a collection in school. I have to donate on the run."

He glanced at my face. "Hey, you're that Hebro kid. That's cool. Here." He fished a dollar out of his pocket.

"Seriously?" I asked. "Thanks!"

He shrugged. "NBD."

Which stands for No Big Deal. But it should really be VBD, for Very Big Deal. Since the big power plant in our town closed down, lots of people lost their jobs. People in Pinewood Bluffs don't have a lot to give.

Errrch! When the bus finally stopped, I jumped off with the big kids. I ran around the high school parking lot, down one sidewalk and up another, straight toward the elementary school doors. I was totally on time!

"Owen Brown — help!"

And I stopped.

Mr. Kenkins, the custodian, was untangling the flagpole ropes. Again.

"Can you give me a hand here?" he asked. "It'll only take one minute."

Brinnnng! The first bell rang.

In three minutes I would be officially late. But when someone says, "Help," how can you refuse? Besides, Mr. Kenkins only asked for one minute. I had three.

As I held up one end of the rope, and Mr. Kenkins worked to unknot the other, I looked out behind the school. The dark pinewoods that gave our town half its name were what remained of one of the oldest forests in the state. Beyond them were ten miles of rocky bluffs that gave us the other half of our name.

Mr. Kenkins unlooped and unthreaded the ropes this way and that until—*brrrinnnnng!*—the late bell rang. Homeroom was starting.

"And . . . done," said Mr. Kenkins with a big smile. "Thanks, Owen."

"Anytime!" I said.

Slamming through the front doors, I found the halls already empty. Argh! I leaped into the main office to grab a late slip off the secretary's desk and toss Maggie's pennies in the collection can.

And I leaped right into the secretary.

"Ahhhh!" she cried.

I spun to keep from knocking her over . . . and spilled Mags's pennies all over the floor.

"Sorry!" I said, fumbling on the floor to

collect them. But I could only find eight blue-haired Lincolns.

Was the missing penny another sign?

"One must have rolled under Principal Carole's door." I stood and reached for the doorknob.

"Don't you dare disturb her!" said the secretary, standing in my way. "Take a late slip."

I dropped Maggie's donation in the collection can, snagged a late slip, and raced toward first period. On the run, I fished out the money my dad and the kid on the bus had given me. I shot the dollar airplanes into Mr. Hemlock's classroom.

"Thanks, O," he called.

I kept running, down the stairs toward homeroom. The guitar case slammed my back with every step. I could picture my grandma wincing, telling me to be more careful with my guitar. She taught me how to play before she died—folk songs, rock songs, everything. My friend Jon Doyle keeps saying that he and I should form a band. But with me on guitar and Jon on triangle—*Strum, bing! Strum, bing!*—I'm not sure you could call it a band.

I tore around the next-to-last corner. Almost there. One final turn, then — *BLAM!* — right into . . . Dana!

The crash threw her into the wall, and I fell flat on my face.

I leaped up and pulled her to her feet. "Dana! I'm such a klutz. Are you okay?"

She looked into my eyes. Her long blonde hair was tangled. Her cheeks were beyond pale. "Owen, I know the real reason my parents went to Iceland. The monsters. They're coming here. But you can't tell a soul, not yet —"

I stepped back. "Monsters? Dana, what are you —"

"Find the book! In my house. It'll tell you everything. You'll know it. It's not like the others."

"Dana —" I thought I heard someone at the far corner. Before I could see who it was, thick black smoke billowed up from the floor under Dana's feet. The air roared like a jet engine. And I heard words — hissing — as if from a million miles away.

The . . . battle . . . begins. . . .

Dana's face went white. "*HELP!*"

She threw something at me. Flames shot up in a ring around her feet, the floor split open, and she fell straight down. I saw eyes, dozens of them. And shiny black stuff. And thrashing shapes. And fire.

"Dana?" I shouted. *"Dana!"*

But an instant later, the floor sealed up, the fire vanished, and Dana was gone.

CHAPTER TWO

DEAD END

"Dana!" I kneeled and hammered my fists on the solid floor, while the school bell ending homeroom jangled on and on. Classrooms emptied, and kids and teachers crowded the hall.

My brain was spinning.

What had just happened was . . . impossible! Had anyone else seen it? Was it just me?

Then I noticed what Dana had thrown at me. Her house key.

Seriously? She wants me to go to her house? To find the book she talked about?

Footsteps pounded toward me. I turned.

It was Jon. "Are you okay? The lights in the whole school blinked out for a second. It was so weird!"

"No," I said. My mouth was dry, and my voice sounded funny.

"It *wasn't* weird?"

"I mean I'm not okay," I said, pointing to the floor. I wasn't sure why, but I lowered my voice, so no one else would hear me. "Dana vanished . . . down there!"

Jon looked at me, then at my feet, then at me again. "Where?"

"Through the floor!" I whispered. "She went *through* the floor! She disappeared! A hole opened up, and she fell into it!"

Jon's jaw dropped. "Mr. Kenkins is going to be so mad. He's too old to fix stuff like that. He even gets tangled in the flagpole ropes—"

I grabbed Jon by the shoulders and gave him a shake. "Jon. Focus. I just saw Dana vanish through

the floor! One second she was here, and the next . . .
poof!"

Jon breathed out, was quiet for a minute, then
nodded. "I get it. I mean, I don't *get* it. But I know
you, Owen. When you say something, you mean it.
What are we going to do?"

That was the thing about Jon. It was sometimes
hard to get his attention. But if you did, he was with
you a hundred percent.

"Stand right here," I said, pointing to the floor tiles.
"I'm going downstairs. Do not move from this spot."

Jon frowned. "This spot? You want me to stand on
the spot where Dana vanished? Is that safe?"

"I'll be right back!" I ran to the end of the hall
and jumped three steps at a time to the lower level.
I knew that there was nothing under the hall except
the boiler room, which was always locked, but I had
to look.

It didn't help. "Dead end," I said to myself, pounding on the iron door.

My heart thudded as I ran back upstairs. Students
and teachers were everywhere now, stepping around

Jon, who was on his hands and knees examining the floor tiles. Tapping her foot on the tiles next to him was a really pale girl with short black hair. She was holding a fire extinguisher.

"Owen, this is Sydney Lamberti," said Jon. "She's a transfer. Her dad's the new shop teacher. She's a real techie. Plus, she smelled smoke."

"You smelled smoke?" I asked the girl. "There was fire. I saw fire coming up from below—"

"I saw it, too," she said. "I was coming around the corner and saw the flames. I freaked out and ran for the fire extinguisher."

"You saw Dana vanish?" I asked her, relieved that I wasn't the only one.

"I saw it, but I don't believe it. Either way," she said, shaking her head, "we should tell someone. The principal. Better yet, let's file a missing person's report. I can do it right now." She pulled out her cell phone.

That's when I remembered. "No!" I grabbed her arm. "Dana told me not to tell anyone. There's some big thing happening. Monsters or something. I know,

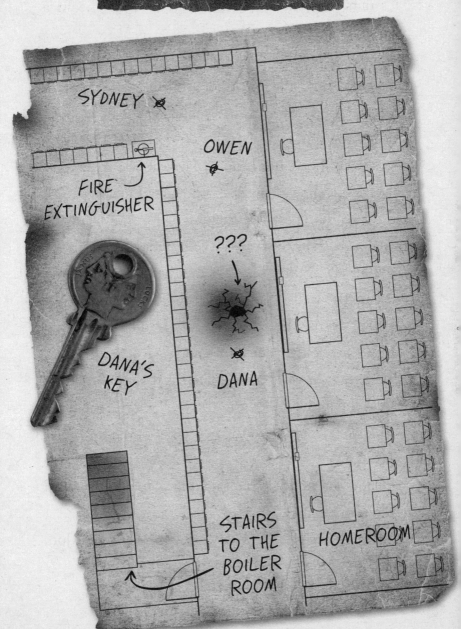

it's nuts. But she was really scared. And I heard a voice. It said, 'The battle begins. . . .'"

"Uh-oh," said Jon. "Not good."

"There were a whole lot of eyes staring at me from below," I said, shivering as I remembered them. "And something shiny . . ."

Sydney shook her head. "Maybe it was a surge of electricity followed by an earthquake. I mean, people just don't disappear like that—"

"Except that we both saw it," I interrupted.

"I know," Sydney said, placing the fire extinguisher next to the wall. "But what can we do about it?"

I felt Dana's house key in my hand. "Dana said there's a book in her house. She gave me her key. She lives near where the concert is this morning. We could slip away. . . ."

I looked from Jon to the new girl, hoping they were with me.

"Hey, I'm totally in," said Jon. "You know that. Dana's our friend."

Sydney peered at the key in my hand, then at Jon,

then at me. She took a breath and said, "I guess I'm in, too. Except that I'm not in the band."

"Do you play an instrument?" Jon asked.

"Gong," she said. "My dad helped me make a gong in shop. Out of bronze."

"You're in the band now!" Jon said.

CHAPTER THREE

THE RUNSON HOUSE

WE COLLECTED OUR INSTRUMENTS — SYDNEY'S gong was a small one she carried in her backpack, anyway — and jammed ourselves into the bus with the other band kids. As we drove away from school, I tried to stay calm. But like everything else that had happened since I woke up, staying calm was impossible, too.

"Guys," I whispered, "something seriously crazy is

going on here. Dana knew she was in danger. I saw it in her eyes. She was terrified."

"Okay, you and I saw her disappear. Fine," said Sydney. "But disappear to where?"

I hadn't even let myself think about *where*. All I could do was shake my head. "I don't know. Somewhere dark. With zillions of eyes and a creepy voice." Not so helpful.

"Which makes it even more important to find the book," said Jon.

When we climbed out at the college, the wind was picking up and the sky was filling with clouds. We pretended to be busy looking through our bags as the other kids hurried into the auditorium to set up for the concert. Soon the bus drove away, and we were alone on the sidewalk.

"So . . . where's Dana's house?" asked Sydney.

I turned to the north. "There. On the hill," I said.

No one noticed as we made our way past the old brick buildings to a high front yard across the street from campus. I'd been to the Runsons' house quite

a few times over the years. It was two hundred years old, four stories high, and had nine gables and dozens of very tall windows.

Jon breathed out. "This place is haunted."

"No such thing," said Sydney, as we climbed the steps. "But I think that we should do this quickly. In and out."

"Maybe I could do the *out* part now," said Jon. "I'll wait out here while you go in?"

"Nice try, but no," I said. I pulled Dana's key from my pocket. The moment I turned the key and pushed the door in, a wave of frigid air swept over us.

Jon stepped back. "Whoa, Iceland much?"

"Dana's parents both teach Icelandic stuff," I said. "Dana told me she knew the real reason her parents went to Iceland. Whatever that means."

"You mean *not* for research?" asked Jon.

I shrugged. "I don't know." I was saying that a lot.

We stepped inside, and the cold surrounded us.

"They probably just turned off the heat for while they're away," said Sydney, being practical. I was learning that was her thing. "It also smells like animals." She wrinkled her nose.

The deeper into the house we went, the colder it got. It felt as if the rooms were refrigerated. The walls glittered with a fine coating of frost. If it hadn't been so dark, we probably would have seen icicles hanging from the door frames. Our breath hung like fog in front of us.

The Runsons had just left today, so how did it get so cold so fast?

"We should be really quick about this," said Sydney, rubbing her arms.

We searched from room to room. Dining room. Living room. Bedrooms. Kitchen. Sheets crusted with frost were draped over the furniture to keep the dust off. They looked like dead bodies. I tried not to be creeped out.

We found no obviously important books anywhere until we entered the Runsons' home office. It was pitch-black, no windows. Feeling around, I found the light switch and flicked it on. A single lamp glowed, putting the far corners of the room in shadow. But we saw what we needed to.

"Uh-oh," said Jon.

The library was lined with floor-to-ceiling book-shelves. At the very top was a high shelf filled with big old vases and pots that looked like they belonged in a museum.

"This will be easy." Sydney snorted as she pulled a leather-bound book from a shelf. "There must be a million priceless books here. How are we supposed to find the right one?"

"Dana told me I'd know it," I said. "There's something about it that's different from the others." But I had no idea what.

We started looking through one book after another. Most of them were written in other languages. Some had letters I couldn't recognize, some had painted pictures. Others were so old, they felt like they might crumble in our hands. There was one shelf with a gap between the books as if one had been pulled out. I hoped that wasn't the book Dana needed.

Just as I was beginning to feel helpless, I turned. And I let out a slow white breath.

"What is it?" asked Jon.

A large desk stood in the shadows at the end of the room.

"I read a story once where there was a clue to the mystery in a desk," I said, stepping across the carpet to it. Like the walls, the desk was covered in a film of speckled frost. And it was very neat—pens, ink pots, pencil cups, stacks of paper—everything in its place. A clay bowl of paper clips stood off to one side. In with the clips was a small brass key. Stepping back from the desk, I saw that one of the drawers had a brass lock.

Sydney saw it, too. "Way too obvious."

"But worth a try," Jon said, bouncing on his toes. "Anything to get out of here."

The key was cold when I picked it up from the bowl. I slipped it into the lock and turned it. *Ping!* The drawer popped out, and my breath caught in my throat. Inside the drawer was a very used copy of a very fat paperback book: *Bulfinch's Mythology.*

"Mythology?" Jon said. "You mean like ogres and unicorns?"

"More like gods and monsters," Sydney said. "When I was little, my parents read me those stories. Do you think this is the book Dana was talking about?"

"It's not like the other books on the shelves. It's cheap," I said. I peeled back the cover and saw Dana's name written inside. "Why would she keep it locked up here and not in her room?"

"Maybe *she* didn't keep it locked up," Sydney said. "Maybe her parents did. To protect it? Maybe —"

Grrrrr.

Jon froze. "I think we woke the dog. . . ."

GRRR! The growling was louder.

"They don't have a dog," I said quietly. My hands and feet were numb. I couldn't tell if it was from the cold, or from the fear that shot through me.

A massive *thing* rose up from the shadows. And up and up. Its head alone was the size of a dog. Then it bared its teeth . . . only they weren't just teeth. They were fangs — long and curved and dripping thick goop. The thing's eyes were deep and black. It wasn't a dog.

It was a wolf.

Some kind of crazy extra-large wolf. with spiky bristles of red fur sticking out like bent wire. The giant beast just stared at us, heaving out the foulest frozen breath imaginable.

Jon flattened against the shelves. "Please let this be a dream. And I wake up far away —"

RRRAAOOO! Flames shot out of the beast's jaws as it leaped high over our heads and landed by the library door. It slammed the door shut, and the house echoed — *doom-doom-doom!* We were trapped.

Scrambling backward, I tripped over Jon's feet and fell to the floor. Maybe I was dizzy with fear, but from that angle the bookshelves looked like only one thing.

A ladder.

Without thinking, I leaped up and swung my arms across the top of the desk. Bowls, pens, paper, everything flew at the wolf.

"Up the shelves!" I cried.

In the second it took for the giant wolf to dodge the junk, we clambered up the dark wooden shelves.

The wolf roared fire again, then jumped at us. I hurled a heavy book at its head. With a cry of pain, the wolf tumbled backward.

We clawed our way up to the top shelf. I heaved one of the vases down over my shoulder. So did Jon. The wolf dodged mine, but Jon's caught it on the snout. It shot another blast of fire.

"There's a heating vent in the corner," Sydney said, grabbing my arm and then pointing.

We crawled across the top shelf to the corner, where an ornate grille stood in the wall. Jon and I kept dropping vases and pots at the wolf, while Sydney pulled a tiny screwdriver from her backpack and began to unscrew the grate.

"Shop teachers' daughters are always prepared," she said under her breath.

The wolf roared again, and the lower shelves burst into flame.

"Sydney!" I cried.

"Got it," she said. She yanked out the grille, threw

it over her shoulder, and we scrambled into the darkness beyond. By the time the wolf clawed its way up the shelves, we were deep into the guts of the house. We crawled through one turn after another until we found a second vent. Together we kicked it out, jumped down onto the dining room table, and got out of the house as fast as we could. I made sure to lock the door behind me.

The wolf was still inside, roaring and all crazy mad. The whole thing seemed unreal, but we couldn't stop to think about it. We ran until we saw our bus in front of the auditorium, and we climbed on, breathless and soaked with sweat.

When I slumped into my seat, my heart was beating like a drum. My veins had turned to ice. My tongue didn't work.

But I still had Dana's book.

CHAPTER FOUR

GODS AND MONSTERS

THE OTHER BAND KIDS DIDN'T LIKE THAT WE HAD skipped the concert. But that hardly sank in. Our ride back to school was pretty much a blur — all because of Dana's book.

It bulged with bookmarks, sticky notes, highlighted passages, dog-eared pages, circled words, and hundreds of notes, scrawled up and down the sides of nearly every page. Dana had practically written a whole other book in the margins.

"This better be the right book," said Jon. "I'm not going back in that creepy house."

"If we actually believe what we saw in that house," said Sydney, "and Dana really did vanish into the floor—"

"We do and she did," I said.

"—then this book may tell us *where* she went. Maybe even something about what you heard."

"'The battle begins,'" I said, shuddering.

Sydney tapped our shoulders and whispered. "Guys, we'll be back at school before we know it, so we should read fast. Let's huddle!" Syd might have seemed a bit snobby at first. But I had to admit that she wasn't so bad.

We started poring over the stories Dana had marked. Some were about gods and goddesses. Others were about heroes and monsters. And not just the usual Greek ones. Norse gods from Scandinavia, like Thor and Odin. Egyptian creatures, like the Phoenix and the Sphinx. Even some of the fables from later in history, like Beowulf the dragon slayer.

One name was circled on every page where it

occurred: Hades, ruler of the ancient Underworld. In the margin next to one passage, Dana had scribbled: "Beware Hades' bargains. . . ."

"I remember Hades from the stories," said Sydney. "He's terrifying. And strict. He has to be because he's the Greek king of the dead."

"I like this guy Jason. He was cool," said Jon, tapping his finger on one page. "Getting an awesome team together for a big quest. Like us, forming a band."

Then I read the story of Argus, a beast in charge of keeping people captive. He had a hundred eyes.

"A hundred eyes?" I said. "Like what I saw under the floor of the school? But that's . . . no . . . that's mythology."

"Argus *is* a monster," Jon pointed out, scanning the rest of the page. "You said Dana talked about monsters. The only way Argus could be stopped was with music. A lullaby."

One story that may have been the most marked up was about the Greek hero Orpheus. Dana's squiggly marks ran up and down the page: in pencil, in pen, in marker. We could barely read the original text.

ARGUS

FENRIR

"This seems really big," I said. "She spent a lot of time here."

"Orpheus was a musician whose wife died and went to Hades' Underworld," said Sydney, reading over my shoulder. "He descended to the Underworld to bring her back."

"I've heard about that one," I said.

Sydney continued. "Hades made a bargain with him. He could lead his wife to our world, as long as he didn't look back to see if she was really following him."

"Let me guess," Jon said. "He looked."

Sydney nodded. "*Whoosh!* Orpheus lost her forever—"

"Yeah, well, we're not losing Dana," I said loudly. "Not like that. And anyway, we don't know where she is. But she can't be in some creepy Underworld. Especially not one under our school."

The kids on the bus quieted and turned to us.

"Ha-ha!" said Sydney. "Nothing to see here!" She ducked her head down and flipped to a pink sticky note in the section about Norse myths. "Lots of monsters here, too. The Midgard Serpent. A scary half-blue lady. And . . . uh-oh."

"What?" I said.

Syd went paler than usual. "Fenrir."

"Somebody you know?" asked Jon.

"Somebody we all know," she said, turning to me. "A big red wolf. Really big. With fur sticking out like wire."

I tried to stay calm. "Does Fenrir breathe fire?"

Sydney scanned the page and nodded slowly. "It's kind of his trademark."

Jon's face drained of color until it matched hers. "So, we're living in a weird fat book?"

My heart was doing a drum solo. A hundred eyes? A red wolf? A trip to the Underworld? Was something *mythological* happening with Dana? No. It was too unbelievable.

We read as much as we could, digging further into the Norse myths, before the bus got back to school. We climbed off just as the bell rang.

"Third period," said Jon. "Time for lunch. I can't

think on an empty stomach. Besides, macaroni special today."

"My brain is macaroni!" I said. "But yeah. Come on."

We entered the halls, following the last of the lunch crowd.

"Mythology or not, book or not," said Sydney, leaning close, "we can't keep this a secret anymore. We have to tell someone about Dana. I should call the police or something—"

"She told Owen not to tell," Jon pointed out.

"Even if we went to the police, what would they say?" I asked. "Someone vanishing? Red wolves breathing fire? Lots of creepy eyes? Old books? No one is going to believe a single word."

By the time we got to the cafeteria, the tables were crammed, and the room was roaring with conversation. The lunch line was empty, so Jon quickly slid three trays onto the counter and pushed them ahead of us. The lunch ladies were standing behind the counter.

"Macaroni special, please," Jon said. "Times three!"

Miss Hilda, the roundest lady, gave us a big smile. "Special, special, and special," she said, pointing to each of us.

But before ladling out any food, one of the others — Miss Lillian — stepped out from behind the counter and closed the lunch line door behind Sydney.

The third lady, Miss Marge, a tiny woman with a snowdrift of white hair tucked under her hairnet, closed the accordion gate between the loud cafeteria and the quiet kitchen.

"Uh . . ." Sydney started, ". . . what's going on?"

The kitchen lights flickered overhead, then went out. Torches magically appeared on the walls, sputtering with blue flames. We stepped back in shock as Hilda, Lillian, and Marge lined up together in front of us. One held a giant spatula, another a long soup ladle, and the third a great big pair of kitchen tongs.

"What exactly is happening?" Jon whispered shakily.

The lunch ladies took one step toward us, stared deep into our eyes, and cried out a single word.

"Hoyo-toho!"

Then they began to morph.

CHAPTER FIVE

LOSING OUR LUNCH

FIRST THE LUNCH LADIES GREW SIX, SEVEN, EIGHT feet tall, their heads nearly touching the ceiling tiles. Then their white aprons dissolved into steel gray armor, and their kitchen tools twisted themselves into gleaming spears—with curved blades on each and fur banners hanging from them. Helmets, big and gray and dented from battle, with razor-sharp wings as large as eagle's wings, closed around their faces.

The three of us just watched, dumbstruck.

In seconds, Miss Hilda, Miss Lillian, and Miss Marge had become giant warrior women. Their armor flashed under the torchlight like fireworks.

"This isn't weird at all," Sydney said, backing up as far as she could go.

It got weirder.

As the three helmets stared down at us, a voice came from the one that covered Miss Hilda's face. "Three hundred and four!"

That was all.

Jon breathed in slowly. "Excuse us, but *what* about 'three hundred and four'? If this is a math problem, I'll need lunch before I can—"

"The . . . page . . . number . . ." Miss Lillian boomed. "In that book you're holding, Owen Brown. Read it. Now."

I tried to ignore how these three could possibly know what book I had, or even what my name was. I almost dropped the book twice on the floor, flipping to page 304. And there it was, in the Norse mythology section, at the bottom of the page. An entry on . . .

"The Valkyrior?" I said.

"That's us, dear," said the lunch lady called Miss Marge. "We prefer 'Valkyries,' but please read it aloud. If you would."

"'The Valkyrior — Valkyries — are warlike women mounted on horses and armed with helmets and spears.'" I stopped. "Uh . . ."

"They work for Odin," Sydney continued, taking the book from me. "They choose who will die in battle. It says, 'Their name means "choosers of the slain." When they ride forth on their errand, their armor sheds a strange flickering light.'"

"Just like it's doing now," Jon whispered.

"Doom Rider, I am named!" said the first. "But you know me as Miss Hilda!"

"They call me Death Maiden!" Miss Lillian said from the depths of her helmet. Her voice echoed in the kitchen as if in a cave.

The eye slits in her helmet blazing like fire, Miss Marge said, "I couldn't decide for the longest time. I do like Marge. It's homey. But in the armor, I call myself Soul Snatcher!"

THE VALKYRIES

"Together, we are the Valkyrïes!" the three women cried out. "Daughters of Odin. Warriors and choosers of death! Hoyo-toho!"

A part of me wanted to laugh out loud. Lunch ladies who work for the Norse god Odin? How could anyone believe that? Then they yanked off their helmets, and their faces were not the plump and pink and happy faces from just moments ago. They were gray, stern, angry . . . and deadly serious.

I coughed up the courage to speak. "Are you here because of Dana Runson?"

"She has been taken to the Underworld," said Death Maiden.

My heart sank.

"No, she was sucked into the floor of our school," said Jon.

Death Maiden looked grimly at him. "Two plus two equals . . ."

I was scared to say it.

"You mean- the entrance to the Underworld is under Pinewood Bluffs Elementary?" I whispered.

Soul Snatcher nodded. "One of the entrances."

"So Dana's . . . dead?" Sydney asked, eyes wide.

"Dead to you," said Death Maiden.

"But how do you know?" I asked.

"We choose who will die," said Doom Rider.

Jon raised his eyebrows. "Is that what the chef's surprise is all about?"

"But we did not choose Dana Runson," continued Doom Rider, ignoring Jon's comment.

"So who did?" I asked.

"That's what the great god Odin sent us here to find out," said Soul Snatcher. "He has known for some time that things in the Underworlds are not right. Someone is causing trouble. There is unrest in Hades' world."

I didn't know whether we should call 9-1-1, run for our lives, or both. Did these crazy women actually know something? Or were they simply lunch ladies who ate too much macaroni special and liked to play dress-up?

"But what does Odin know about Hades?" I asked. "Aren't they from different myths?"

"Everyone knows Hades," said Doom Rider. "The

Greek kingdom of the dead is the largest of the Underworlds."

"You keep saying Underworlds, plural," said Sydney. "How many are there?"

"One for every branch of mythology," said Miss Marge. "They share space down below. Sometimes . . . uneasily. You have already seen a monster, have you not?"

Jon gasped. "Fenster, a wolf the size of a horse!"

"Fenrir, the Norse monster wolf," Death Maiden corrected him. "He may be the first beast to have escaped the Underworlds. He will not be the last."

"Fenrir is the pet of Loki, the Norse trickster god," said Doom Rider. "Odin and Loki have quarreled for centuries."

"What does all this have to do with Dana?" I asked, shaking my head.

Miss Hilda leaned down at us. "The battle is beginning. You know this already, Owen Brown. You were with Dana when she was taken. You gazed upon Hades' kingdom."

I remembered the fiery pit. "Other monsters were

thrashing around there. I think I saw the one called Argus. Are you saying that more monsters are coming?"

Miss Hilda's eyes fixed on me. "I am saying the battle has begun, Owen Brown."

"I'm not a fighter," I said, stepping back.

Miss Hilda leaned even closer. "All your H.E.R.O. charities? Your love of people? You fight for what's right, don't you?"

"Well, sure, I try, but . . ."

"Try harder," said Death Maiden.

"Try more," said Soul Catcher.

"Try now!" they all said together.

Miss Hilda pointed her spear out the kitchen windows. "There is one weapon that may help you."

"A sword?" asked Sydney. "Does it have a cool name, like Demon Biter or Chopper or—"

"It is a stringed instrument," said Doom Rider.

Sydney and Jon turned to me. "That's your department," they said together.

"The lyre of Orpheus," Soul Snatcher added. "It's like a small harp." She spread her hands about twelve inches apart. "The music of Orpheus's lyre could charm people and beasts to do his bidding. Even trees bowed at the sound of it. Travelers to the Underworlds might find it very . . . useful."

"Travelers to . . ." I didn't want to understand what she meant. "We're supposed to—"

"Retrieve your destiny!" boomed Miss Hilda. "Enter the double red doors! Walk among the ancient things. And remember . . . three!"

"Fifty!" said Soul Snatcher.

"One hundred!" said Death Maiden.

"Is this math again?" asked Jon.

"Or a riddle?" Sydney added.

"A riddle, dear," said Soul Snatcher with a chuckle. "We're ladies from mythology, so we have to speak in riddles. It's one of the most charming things about us!"

Then the three Valkyries sang out again.

"*Hoyo-toho!*"

The torches vanished, the lights came up, their armor became aprons again, and their spears turned back into kitchen utensils. They used them to dollop macaroni specials on each of our plates.

Then Miss Hilda smiled and said, "Shoo — lunch period's nearly over!"

CHAPTER SIX

BEYOND THE DOUBLE DOORS

WE STUMBLED TO A HALF-EMPTY TABLE WITH OUR trays and pulled our chairs close.

"So, are we ready to call the cops yet?" asked Jon.

"Or the loony bin?" asked Sydney. "Maybe we can get a deal. Three for one."

I made a face at her. "Who are you talking about—us or the lunch ladies?"

Sydney had the book now and was flipping its pages with one hand while she forked up macaroni with the other. "To borrow a line from you, Owen, I don't know." She was quiet for a minute, thinking. "I mean, we *did* see a fire-breathing wolf."

"We did," Jon said.

"And Dana *did* vanish," she added.

"She did," I said.

"And if those ladies . . ." Sydney paused to look toward the kitchen. "If those ladies really *are* the Valkyries from Norse mythology, what they told us might be true."

"If. Might," I echoed, stabbing my macaroni a little harder than I planned. "Are you saying Dana was actually taken to the Underworld? And that the Underworld is below our school?"

The other kids at the table looked over at me. Oops.

"Ha-ha! Still kidding!" said Jon.

"Listen," said Sydney, whispering now. "Where do they have double red doors? And ancient things? Guys, I think we need to learn more about Orpheus's lyre. Let's finish eating and go to the library."

I nodded. "The farther we get away from the kitchen, the better I'll feel."

We cleared our trays and ran upstairs. Plunking down at the first open computer, we logged in and started searching.

"Orpheus. Lyre. Red doors. Ancient things," said Sydney, clacking away on the keys.

I paced back and forth, but it was less than a minute before she and Jon were cupping their hands over their mouths.

"Whoa!" Sydney said. "The art museum in town has an exhibit that's closing . . . today. It's called 'Ancient Treasures.' And the picture of the museum here shows that it has — ta-da! — double red doors!"

As Sydney scrolled down and I paced, Jon read over her shoulder. "It's got swords. Shields. Scrolls. Jeweled stuff. And stop . . . stop . . ."

"Owen!" said Sydney, staring from the screen to me. "You'll never believe —"

I stopped pacing. "The lyre of Orpheus?"

"Yes!" Sydney said. "The lyre is part of the exhibit

leaving the museum today. Its next stop is another museum in . . ."

I held my breath as she scrolled to the bottom of the page. She raised her face to me, her eyes wide.

"Iceland!" she said.

I felt as cold as if *I* were in Iceland.

"The lunch ladies want us to steal the lyre of Orpheus? Seriously?" asked Jon.

"Orpheus's lyre is one of the most powerful objects of the ancient world," Sydney said. "Maybe it'll help us get Dana back."

That was it, wasn't it? We had to help Dana.

"The museum is five blocks from here," I said. "We can walk, but we'll need to get out of school for the afternoon."

Jon groaned. "Never gonna happen."

But Sydney jumped up from the computer and grinned. "My dad's the shop teacher, don't forget. He can give us a pass."

We looked at one another. I didn't like lying, but this was different. If there *was* something mytho- logical and magical and weird going on, no one was going to believe us. Dana would still be gone. Maybe gone for good. We had to do something.

"Next stop, shop class!" I said, marching out of the library.

༄ ༄ ༄ ༄ ༄

It turned out that Mr. Lamberti was a nice guy. A nice guy who didn't ask a lot of questions.

Ten minutes later, we were staring up at a small, white granite building with a set of large red doors. Marble columns at least twenty feet tall stood across the front of the museum like warriors at attention. It was an imitation of a Greek temple, which seemed completely right.

And scary.

We raced up the steps and through the doors, paid admission, and walked as fast as we could to the exhibit. It was curtained off, but we peeked in. Several guards and a couple of curators in suits were moving around from display to display with clipboards, checking things off, pointing.

"They're getting ready to ship it out," Sydney whispered.

We slipped behind one heavy curtain and peeked out to scan the long room.

After talking to the Valkyries, some things were beginning to make sense in my mind: Get the lyre. Go to the Underworld. (Well, one of the Underworlds.) Save Dana.

Yeah, right. The whole thing was nuts. Completely. But despite all that, things were starting to click in my head.

No, not click.

Hum.

"There are a dozen display cases with instruments in them," Sydney whispered. "How do we know which one has the—"

"Second one from the end," I said, pointing.

My friends stared at me. Maybe it was all those years at my grandma's house, learning how to play guitar, feeling music in my fingers. Maybe it wasn't me at all, but the lyre. Miss Marge told us it was magical. And powerful. Whatever the reason, I *heard* the lyre. And apparently no one else could.

Thrummm . . .

"Owen, are you receiving signals from the beyond?" whispered Sydney.

"No, from that case at the end of the room," I said. "The lyre's in there. We need to get closer."

"And get ourselves arrested!" Jon said.

I knew it was crazy. But so was what I had seen happen to Dana that morning.

Thrummm . . .

"Follow me," I whispered.

As if I suddenly knew what I was doing, I ducked back behind the curtain and ran out to the far end of the hall, peering in the door closest to the case. Jon and Sydney followed and crouched next to me.

Two workers came over to the case. One inserted a key, and the other tilted the glass back. As he did, the sound grew louder in my ears. *Thrummm, thrummm.* It was like someone urging me, "Owen, come on!" Slipping on a pair of white gloves, the curator lifted the lyre. I drew in a breath. That was it!

It was a wooden horseshoe a foot square and painted gold, though most of its paint had flecked off. A crossbar connected the two arms of the U, with

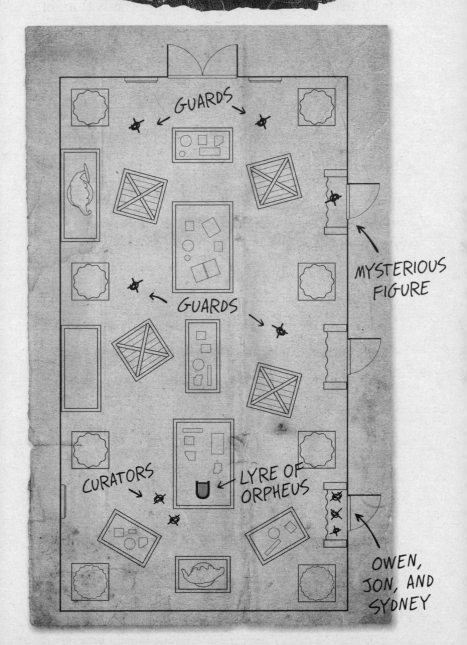

ANCIENT TREASURES EXHIBIT

GUARDS

MYSTERIOUS FIGURE

GUARDS

CURATORS

LYRE OF ORPHEUS

OWEN, JON, AND SYDNEY

seven strings stretched between it and the bottom of the U.

Jon gave me a nudge. "Owen, stop drooling over that thing and look over there."

A lone figure in a dark coat was lurking behind the curtain we had just abandoned. He wore thick black headphones over his ears. He crept closer and stopped. I began to sweat. Maybe it wasn't just gods and monsters. Maybe there were people involved in this mystery, too.

"Who's he?" whispered Sydney.

"Someone else who doesn't want to be seen?" said Jon. "Someone who wants to steal the lyre, too? We should probably get out of here—"

But the man with the headphones was blocking our one escape route. Everywhere else, there were more guards than we could deal with. We were trapped.

The moment the curator set the lyre in a wooden box, the thing hummed in my ears again, and Soul Snatcher's words came back: *The music of Orpheus's lyre could charm people and beasts to do his bidding.*

Impossible, right? But I heard the lyre. Did that mean it could actually work? And could it work for me?

Quickly forming a plan, I jumped out of hiding and grabbed the lyre from the box. "I need this!" I shouted.

"Owen!" cried Sydney, reaching for me.

All the lights went up and the man with the headphones ducked back behind the curtain. I heard him running off down the hall.

Guards swarmed over us in seconds. "Who are you?" they yelled. "Up against the wall!"

"Put down that lyre!" said a curator. "Gently, please—"

"I think you'd better plug your ears," I whispered to Jon and Sydney as I placed my fingers on three of the seven strings. "Don't ask why. Now!"

As they jammed their fingers in their ears, I turned to the curator. "You mean *this* lyre?"

I plucked the strings.

Brum-thru-lummmm!

The three strings vibrated, and the world around

me quieted. Everything slowed down — things moved so little that I thought time had stopped. The moment passed, and just after it did, I watched the guards drop their arms to their sides.

"That's my favorite tune!" one said, smiling.

"Mine, too," said another, closing his eyes.

I brushed the strings again, and the chief guard said, "You kids better get back to school. The side entrance is the quickest way out."

"What about the lyre?" I asked.

"You play it so nicely," said the curator. "Try it for a few days. If you like it, keep it."

So. The lyre *was* magical. It could make people do things on command, ridiculous things. And for some reason, I knew how to use it.

"Okay, then," I said. "Bye!"

Fingers still in their ears, Jon and Sydney stumbled after me down the hall to the museum doors, and soon we were out on the front steps — with the lyre. No one chased us. No alarm blared. Nothing.

"How did you do that?" Jon blurted, finally unplugging his ears.

"I didn't," I said. "The lyre did. It has amazing powers. The thief knows it, too. I bet he was wearing those big headphones to block the lyre's sound." I looked down at the magical instrument in my hands. "Look, if Dana was taken to the Underworld — no matter how or why — school is where it happened. The Valkyries said that the entrance is under the school. So that's where we need to be. With this."

"We'd better hurry," said Sydney, checking her cell. "Dismissal's in eight minutes. Our parents . . ."

We ran as fast as we could and arrived at school just as the buses were pulling out. I saw my mom waiting in her car, and headed over to her.

"Owen," she said, getting out and looking annoyed. "I just saw Mr. Lamberti, and he told me you were all gone from school. What's going on? Why isn't Dana with you?"

I drew in a slow breath to calm myself and glanced at Jon and Syd. "Mom, I can explain everything. Listen . . ."

Jon and Sydney slapped their hands over their ears just in time, as the lyre's strings moved under my fingers. "We're all staying after school. Dana is . . . inside. We're doing some extra credit. I mean, if that's okay with you . . ."

I knew it was wrong, but when Mom's expression went from annoyed to interested to happy, it seemed like the right thing to do.

"Pretty little harp," Mom said, smiling. "Reminds me of your grandmother."

"Me, too," I said. "Mom, we're going back into school now. Dana and I will be home for dinner. Promise."

Mom nodded and grinned from ear to ear. "See you then!"

I hoped I wouldn't have to break my promise.

CHAPTER SEVEN

THE BOILER ROOM

I FIGURED THAT THE EFFECTS OF THE LYRE WOULD eventually fade, and people would go back to normal again, so I kept plucking the strings until my mom drove down the street and I couldn't see her anymore.

"That lyre is some kind of magic weapon," Jon said.

"I'm totally going to invent us some super earplugs," Sydney added.

I turned to them. I had a vague idea of what we were about to do, and it seemed completely crazy and probably dangerous. "You realize this is all nuts, right? The Underworlds. The lunch ladies. The weirdo big wolf. The magic lyre. This whole mythological thing."

"Like we've been eating crazy pudding," said Jon.

"Except we don't really have a choice," said Sydney.

"Exactly," I said. "Just so we're all on the same page about it."

The school was unlocked, which wasn't strange. What *was* strange was that the instant we stepped inside, the public address system crackled.

"Owen Brown, report to the office!"

"Why is the office still open?" asked Jon. "And how does anyone know we're here?"

When we got to the main office, we found the secretary standing at the door with her coat on, ready to leave.

"Here," she said, dropping something into my palm.

"The penny!" I said, peering down at it. "You found Mags's penny with blue Lincoln hair!"

The secretary smiled. "Under the principal's desk.

The collection can is in the safe for the night and won't be out again until the morning. If you want, you can bring this back then." She switched off the office lights, shooed us into the hall, and left the building with a wave.

"Nice little moment," said Sydney. "But we have an Underworld to get to."

"And a Dana to save," said Jon.

I tucked the penny into my pocket. "Let's go."

We entered the maze of hallways toward the back of the school. The lyre glowed eerily under the ceiling lights. Our footsteps echoed off the walls. There was a smell, too. Not coffee from the teachers' lounge. Not mashed potatoes from the cafeteria. Not cleaning fluid from the janitor's closet. It was the same thing I had smelled when Dana disappeared.

"Smoke," I said under my breath.

We took the stairs carefully and quietly, but I couldn't stop the panic in my chest. Was there really an entrance to the Underworlds below our school? Would the lyre help us get into it? And out of it? Was any of this *real*?

"It's locked," said Sydney when we got to the boiler room door. "No way can I open this with my tool kit."

"Maybe the lyre can do it," said Jon. "Orpheus charmed rocks and dead stuff, too."

"I'm not Orpheus," I said, feeling unworthy of the ancient magical instrument in my hands.

But I tried it, anyway. For a reason I can't explain, my fingers went right to the two highest pitched of the seven strings. I plucked them one after another, making a simple two-note melody. Even before the notes faded, the door began to quiver like the surface of a pond. It turned gray, then silver, then white.

Then it wasn't there.

"Whoa!" Jon whispered. "You're the Jimi Hendrix of the ancient lyre!"

Probably not.

But instead of furnaces and pipes and cables and machines behind the boiler room door, we saw charred trees and giant boulders surrounded by hills of rough black earth. The sky, if that's what the ceiling of the boiler room had become, stormed with fiery clouds.

I went cold all over. This couldn't be true. This was beyond impossible. It was terrifying.

We stood on the edge of the creepy landscape, staring and unable to move, until we heard the soft lapping of water.

"Dana's book tells about a river dividing the living and dead," Syd said softly. "You have to cross it to get to the land of the dead. It's called the river Styx."

Jon whistled. "If Mr. Kenkins only knew what was in his boiler room."

"Dana's in there somewhere," I said, trying to sound strong. "Come on." We followed the sound of the water down a steep, black slope to an area of overgrown reeds. The rank smell of a polluted river filled the air. Then the reeds moved, and an ancient man in a droopy hat limped slowly toward us, leaning on a long wooden pole.

Before I could do anything, I felt Jon and Sydney move to stand quietly behind me.

The old man stopped and tipped his hat.

"I am Charon. At your service," he said. His voice sounded like gravel rolling in a tin can.

"You're the ferryman, aren't you?" I asked, my words trembling. "We read about you."

Charon licked his lips when he saw the lyre. "I've seen that before. Long ago."

"We need to get across the river," said Sydney, peeking out from behind my shoulder. "I mean, sort of, you know . . . please?" It was the first time I'd seen Sydney choke a little. My own fears doubled.

Charon kept his eyes on the lyre. "This way," he said. He turned and hobbled a short distance to the river, then paused. "Will you be wanting a round-trip, like Orpheus? Or one-way?"

"Round-trip!" said Jon quickly.

Charon snorted. "Optimistic, aren't you? Well, come on. Climb aboard the yacht."

Tucked among the reeds was *not* a yacht. It was a raft of soggy planks tied together with frayed rope. When we stepped on, the thing nearly tipped over. But when Charon climbed on, the raft didn't make the slightest dip in the water. The old man had no weight.

"Hold tight," he said, showing two rows of black gums with not a single tooth. "Lest you fall among *them*. They're grabby, you know."

Jon tugged my sleeve. "*Who's* grabby?"

I didn't know, but when Charon pushed his pole against the shore and the raft floated into the river, we saw *them*—human shapes swimming under the waves, their mouths open in silent screams.

"The recent dead," Charon explained. "They haunt the shore, hoping to rejoin the living, fearing to cross to the far side."

"What will happen to them?" Sydney asked.

"They'll cross," Charon said darkly. "They all do."

I thought about my grandmother. It had been so hard when she'd died two years ago. She wasn't even that old. Then she was gone. Would I see her here? Would we see *all* the dead here? The idea made me shiver, and I clutched the lyre more tightly.

Soon we left the shallow waters and the silent souls. For minutes, the only sound was the waves

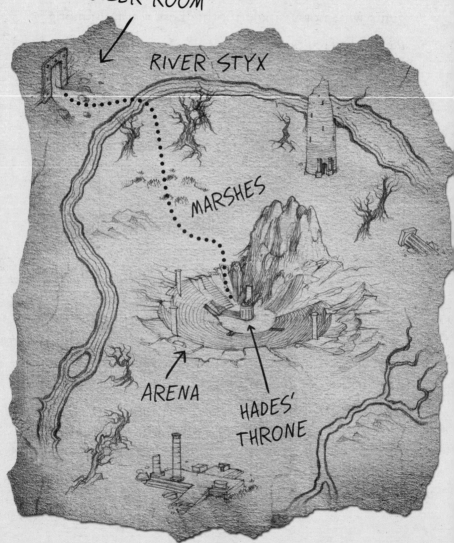

THE GREEK UNDERWORLD

BOILER ROOM

RIVER STYX

MARSHES

ARENA

HADES' THRONE

lapping over the planks. Before long, we docked among the reeds on the dead side and got off the raft one by one. Then Charon thrust his hand out at me, palm up.

"A little something?" he asked.

I gulped. I had given everything to the charities that morning.

Sydney and Jon shook their heads at me.

Charon's old eyes flashed with anger. He turned away. "One-way voyage, then."

"But we have to get home!" said Jon.

"No exceptions," said Charon.

"The penny!" Sydney whispered. "With the blue hair!"

I dug into my pocket, pulled out Mags's penny, and dropped it into Charon's palm.

He grinned. "If you come back after work hours, you'll stay here, which means bye-bye to your old lives. No one leaves after I go off duty. Five P.M." Tipping his filthy hat once more, he waded among the tall reeds and disappeared.

"This is way scarier than the Runson house," Jon muttered.

We started walking up a rising slope of coal black ground dotted with leafless dead trees. It took us a few minutes to get to the top, where we found ourselves overlooking an enormous arena. It stretched for miles end to end and contained benches filled with millions of hooded, silent figures, who sat stiff and unmoving.

I couldn't believe it. "The dead," I said. "So many of them . . ."

At the near end of the arena stood what looked like the back of a throne, twenty feet high.

"Someone's big," Jon said under his breath.

Syd gasped softly. "That must be Hades' throne! The king of the Greek dead would have a huge throne. Oh, man . . ."

There was a long flight of stairs down to the throne. "This is for Dana, remember," I said, setting my foot on the top step. But the moment I did — *whoosh!* — the stairs became a slide. We slammed onto our backs and shot all the way down the arena to the bottom.

The instant we landed, the giant throne swung around to us, and my heart stopped.

In the throne sat an enormous beast.

It was shaped like a man, but its skin was as red as a stop sign, and it wore gleaming bloodred armor from shoulders to feet. Its head was a mess of wild flaming horns twisting out of its skin like a thicket. Its eye sockets were as wide as dinner plates and as hollow as tunnels, except for white flames blazing in each.

And when it spoke, the air shook.

"Welcome to my Underworld!"

CHAPTER EIGHT

KING, MONARCH, RULER

"ALLOW ME TO INTRODUCE MYSELF," SAID THE GIANT red beast. "My name is Hades."

We all knew who he was. We had heard about him from the Valkyries and read about him in Dana's overstuffed book. We had probably known about him since we were small. Every mythology had a Death King, and Hades was a mighty one.

"You must be tired from your long and, no doubt,

strange journey," Hades said. "Take a rest. Here. By me." He patted the arms of his giant throne. "Come, sit . . ."

At every word, mist rose from his mouth like breath in the winter. Only it wasn't human breath. It was smoke, thick and gray and smelling of death.

"Why so standoffish?" he asked, his red armor gleaming.

We didn't move. We were too scared.

But I managed to cough out a few words.

"She's here," I said. "Dana Runson."

Hades slapped his knees and roared with laughter. "Getting right to the point!"

His laughter ended as suddenly as it began. His smile died. He stared from one to the other of us in terrifying silence.

Jon and Sydney took up their usual position behind me. I could hear them breathing. It felt good to have them that close.

I gripped the lyre tightly, and its strings pressed into my arms. I had no idea if it would work on

Hades, as the legends said it had for Orpheus. I was no Orpheus. And that scared me even more. But we had no choice. We came for one reason.

"Dana Runson," I said. "We want her back."

This time, Hades put on a sad face. "And she's *here*, you say? Well, that *is* too bad." He paused to summon one of the hooded shapes. It drifted over to the throne, and Hades leaned down as it whispered into his ear. He listened, then waved the shape away. "Was this Dana Runson young? I know it hurts you humans when your friends die young."

"She didn't die," Sydney said, staring up at Hades. "We're pretty sure you took her."

I was glad she said it, so I didn't have to.

Hades' eyes turned as black as the river we had just crossed. He allowed himself to look at the lyre for the first time. "I see you've got Orpheus's old noisemaker. I won't ask where you found it."

"It's the real one," said Jon.

"Oh, I know it is," said Hades. "Do you have any idea of the power it possesses?"

I swallowed. "We're here, aren't we?"

Hades' eyes narrowed. "Except that it's far easier to *enter* my Underworld than it is to *leave* it. In fact, in the whole history of my kingdom, only a few ever made the return journey. The entrances to the Underworld are many. The exits are few. You've been lucky enough to find an opening that is both. Yet, this is the Underworld. It's like the name. Your friend has gone *under*. She's lost to you."

It felt like my heart was trying to beat its way up to my throat. "Dana isn't lost. She was kidnapped. She shouldn't be here—"

"Kidnapped!" Hades boomed, standing to his full terrifying height. "I run a tidy ship, little humans! If *someone* has fooled with the entrances and exits of *my* world, I shall discover it! If anyone has violated my laws, I shall take action!"

His words echoed around and around the arena. When they finally drifted away, Sydney raised her hand. "Sir, the Valkyries told us something was going on. And we saw a wolf. Fenrir—"

Grrr . . . grrrr . . . grrrrr. Several animals growled behind the giant throne.

Hades looked down suddenly and sat again. "Ooh, did the dogs hear a name they don't like?" he said. "*Hmm?* Fenrir is not here, my little friends. Come out. Come out!"

A hideous, black-furred head emerged from the darkness behind the throne. It was the size of a garbage can. A second head swung out after it, its fur silver white. A third ugly head lolled between the first two, nearly furless, with swollen eyes, its red snout battered and scarred. The heads were connected.

"Cerberus," Sydney whispered, tapping the cover of Dana's book. "He's in here, too. The three-headed dog. The lunch ladies said to look out for three, fifty, and a hundred. Could this be the *three*?"

Hades gave us a cold grin. "I call the poor middle one Anger, because the other two take his food. This makes him lean and hungry. Beware all three of them, but most of all beware Anger. He is slow to eat but quick to fight."

I couldn't believe I was standing in the Underworld, talking to Hades. I couldn't believe I was standing in front of his three-headed dog.

I couldn't believe I was standing.

Then I remembered Miss Hilda's question. *You fight for what's right, don't you?*

"Dana," I repeated. "We want to bring her home. We have to. Now."

Hades looked directly at me with his flaming eyes. "If your friend was brought here illegally, I will know it soon. In the meantime, a little bargain . . ."

I remembered Dana's words. *Beware Hades' bargains.*

Hades rolled an object nearly as tall as himself from the shadows. It was an ancient hourglass. Black sand poured from the top into the bottom.

He tapped the glass and stared at me. I tried to hold his gaze. "I'll let you take your friend back. But there are rules: You have to find her first. You have the lyre. It worked for Orpheus . . . more or less." He looked off into the distance. "Your friend is not far, being held like all newcomers. There's a plain. A big mud hill. A tower. You have an hour to find her. Let's see what you're made of."

"So this is a test?" Jon said.

Hades' eyes burned white. "Everything is a test! The question is, have you studied? Now go! GO! GO!"

Suddenly, the arena erupted with angry voices. "Go! Go!" chanted the millions of hooded figures all around us. Their voices roared louder and louder as their bony hands pointed beyond the arena.

Cerberus's three heads growled at us and strained at their leashes while Hades summoned more hooded shapes to him, his face grim.

We had no choice.

Shadows fell over us like lead helmets as we entered the darkness behind Hades' throne.

CHAPTER NINE

THE BRONZE TOWER

THE AIR BEYOND HADES' ARENA WAS AS THICK AS smoke. It stunk like burning trash. We groped our way forward in near darkness.

But no matter how deep into the gloom we walked, we could still hear each grain of black sand falling into the bottom of the hourglass.

"How long do we have?" asked Jon.

"I don't know," I said. "All I know is that I don't

trust Hades. We need to hurry before he changes his mind."

Finally, the smoke cleared a little, allowing us a view of black earth as far as the eye could see, dotted by burned tree stumps and black-water marshes. The smell didn't let up.

Sydney pointed ahead. "Look."

A strange, ragged-looking tower stood on a rise in the distance. It was made of dull brown metal streaked with green.

"That's bronze," said Sydney, "like my gong."

Just in front of the bronze tower was a huge mound of dirt. It rose to a point at the top.

"I guess that's the big mud thing Hades told us about," said Jon. "It looks like a volcano."

I tightened my grip on the lyre and felt my stomach flip-flop. "If Cerberus was *three*, we have to expect *fifty* and a *hundred* of something soon. Everyone ready?"

Step by step we crossed the plain, weaving around the soggy marshes, across the black ground, to the base of the dirt mound. It stood tall and silent and dark. We made our way completely around it, until the bronze tower loomed in front of us.

"That was surprisingly easy," Syd whispered.

"Why are you whispering?" asked Jon.

"Because I'm scared—" She stopped.

We heard a sound. Like a *shhh* followed by a *thud*.

We turned around. A man stood next to the big mud hill, wearing a suit of gleaming black armor. But it wasn't regular armor. It was rounded and knobby, like the shell of a giant insect. The man must have been eight feet tall, and his helmet was a great black bulb, with a narrow slit for an eyehole. On the center of his helmet was the letter M, blazing in red.

In his hands, he held an ax the size of me.

"And that's what I'm scared of," Sydney said, echoing what we all felt.

My fingers already ached from clutching the lyre, but I tightened my grip even more. "I saw that armor," I said. "When Dana disappeared."

Shhh . . . thud. A second man appeared.

"I think I know where this is heading," Jon muttered, backing up.

Shhh . . . thud. Shhh . . . thud. Another and another appeared, sliding down from a hole at the top of the mud house. Before we knew it, the ground was covered with black-armored, ax-wielding warriors. When they stopped, I did a quick scan. "Fifty. There are fifty of them."

"And the lunch ladies score again," said Jon.

"At least there aren't a hundred," Sydney added, then she gasped. "Wait . . . M . . . M . . . big warriors . . . oh, no, no, no!" She flipped the pages of Dana's book. "I bet those are the Myrmidons!"

Jon backed up. "The *friendly* Myrmidons?" he asked hopefully.

"They're known as great warriors," she said. "Huge. Fearless. They must be guarding the bronze tower from people like us."

We watched, stunned, as the Myrmidons assembled into a wall of black armor in front of their mud house. Fifty strong, they stood at attention about twenty feet from us. Then they all stepped forward at once.

THUD. The ground shook.

"Owen," said Sydney, "play something helpful. And loud!" She and Jon clapped their hands over their ears.

I slammed the lyre like an air guitar. *Brannng!* Notes twanged and echoed between the mud house and the bronze tower.

THUD! The Myrmidons advanced again like a single iron machine.

"They don't hear it!" cried Jon. "Their helmets are too thick. Or their brains are. Let's get into that tower!"

We turned and ran for the tower doors, then stopped short, almost plunging into a chasm that ran around the tower like a moat. The pit was too deep and wide to jump across.

"You've got to be kidding," Sydney said.

THUD! The Myrmidons advanced again.

"We're trapped," said Jon. "We're going to die here. Dana will die here. It's all over —"

"Shh!" said Sydney, her nose deep in Dana's book. "There's a story about a plague that took the lives of

almost everyone in a kingdom. Seeing an army of black ants near an oak tree, the king asked Zeus for as many citizens as ants—"

"What does this have to do with us dying here?" Jon squeaked in a panic.

"Listen!" Syd said. "Zeus turned those black ants into warriors. The king called them Myrmidons, because *myrmex* means 'ants'! Those warriors are ant men!"

"Ant men?" Jon said. He turned to face the giant, advancing warriors. "Get back to your dumb anthill!"

Typical Jon. But it gave me an idea.

THUD! Another step.

Even if the Myrmidons were deaf to the lyre, maybe their anthill wasn't. As the black-armored men advanced yet again, I hit the strings one by one, hoping to find the right combination. The third string twanged oddly. Its sound coiled up over my head . . . and the giant mud house began to quiver behind the warriors. I kept plucking the string until a chunk of mud slid from the top and began to roll down. It picked up more mud on the way to the bottom. It grew bigger and bigger. Before long, it was bigger than the warriors.

"Incoming mud ball!" shouted Jon.

When the ball of mud reached the bottom of the hill, it crashed through the ranks of the Myrmidons from behind, scattering them like bowling pins. It kept rolling all the way toward the tower. Then it came upon the pit and stopped dead, lodged between the two sides.

"There's our bridge!" I shouted.

As the warriors regrouped, the three of us clambered across the top of the mud ball to the base of the tower. With another twang of the lyre, I made the bronze doors fly open. We rushed inside.

"That lyre is the best weapon!" Jon said.

"Except"—Sydney pointed behind us—"they're still coming."

The Myrmidons reassembled and began climbing over the mud ball after us.

"Shut the doors!" Sydney cried out. But as soon as we slammed the heavy doors and lowered a massive bronze beam into place, iron fists shook the tower.

An instant later, one of the door hinges popped and flew across the room.

"Jon, help me find something else to secure the doors!" said Sydney. "Owen, go! Find Dana!"

I turned. A narrow circular staircase coiled up from the center of the floor.

"Go!" yelled Jon.

I raced up the stairs as fast as I could. They led up and out to the roof of the tower. All around me were open ramparts. The sky was black overhead. In the very center of the tower roof was a prison made of frosted glass. My heart skipped.

Dana stood motionless behind the glass. My friend, Dana. Imprisoned in the Underworld. My hands shook, and my knees felt like jelly.

She was dressed in a silvery toga, and her eyes were closed as if she were asleep. Or as if she were . . .

"Dana?" I said. "Please . . . Dana . . ."

She didn't answer. But someone else did.

"No one passes Argus, guardian of the newly arrived!"

A blubbery beast slithered out from behind the

glass prison. It was the basic shape of a person, with massive arms and hands of pure muscle, but he was covered from head to feet with eyeballs. Without thinking, I knew there were a hundred eyes. The final piece of the Valkyries' puzzle. The eyes rolled all over the place, until they focused on me.

My heart sank like the black sand in the hourglass. It was the monster and me. Only me. If I failed, would Dana be stuck here forever? Who would be next? Us?

"I've seen you before," I said, backing slowly away from the beast. "When Dana was kidnapped—"

"I see you a hundredfold!" said Argus, sliding closer to me. The hole he talked from was lined with blubbery gums that dripped thick liquid. When Argus spoke, he blasted spit and disgusting breath. "Now, human, prepare to—"

"Ugly beast!" I yelled. I dragged my fingernails across the lyre strings, and Argus laughed.

"Your harsh music merely tickles me!" he boomed. "My new Dark Master will not be crossed! Prepare to suffer our wrath, puny boy!"

Dark Master?

The many-eyed beast slid his way closer, belching and drooling. Backing up, I remembered the story of how Argus was defeated—not by strength but by being lulled to sleep by music.

I gently brushed the strings. *Blummm . . . frummm . . .*

"Sleep," I said. "Sleep . . ."

"What? No! Master, come—" Argus cried, flailing his great big paws at me. But with a loud rush of foul air, his hundred eyes began to roll up into his blubbery flesh, one by one. Finally, all hundred eyes were closed.

Without a minute to waste, I turned around and slammed the lyre's strings—hard. Dana's glass prison shattered into a million crystals. She stood like a statue, frozen, dead. Her eyes were closed. Frost dusted her cheeks like glitter. For an instant, I thought I was too late. She was so pale, so cold.

I took her hand. "Dana, please wake up. We're going to take you home—"

I heard the sound of bronze shattering below. A

scream. Armored feet thudded across the floor. The stairs squealed with heavy steps. Then Sydney's cry. "Owen! Owen —"

Dana's eyelids fluttered.

"Dana?" I whispered.

She gulped a huge breath.

"Say something," I said.

Her lips parted. "Owen . . . behind you!"

I spun around. A giant Myrmidon burst out onto the ramparts. With a single blow, he knocked me down and sent the lyre skidding across the tower floor.

CHAPTER TEN

THE VERY BIG DEAL

I SLAMMED TO THE TOWER FLOOR HARD, ROLLED once, and grabbed the flying lyre before it tumbled to the ground below. Glancing up, I saw Sydney and Jon clambering out to the roof and throwing themselves at the giant Myrmidon. His legs were massive. It took both of them hanging on to a single knee to bring him down.

But down he went — like an anvil — into the sleeping lump of Argus. He bounced off the blubbery beast . . . and straight off the side of the tower. Argus woke with a high-pitched squeal and a belch. Great.

"Face me now!" he cried, thundering toward us.

"Oh, come on!" I played the lullaby again. Argus moaned once and shrank away from the stairs. "Guys, let's go!" I yelled to Sydney and Jon.

"Not ssso fast!" hissed a distant voice. "Myrmidonsss, rise! Finish them!"

I swung around to see a terrifying shape leap up from the base of the tower and land heavily. It was Fenrir, the giant red wolf. It reared high on its hind legs and blasted the air with fire. On its back sat a huge figure—a man of ice, frost, and smoke. Steam curled up from his face, obscuring his features, while also forming horns that twisted as if they were alive.

"Interloperssss!" the figure hissed. "Troublemakerssss! The girl is mine!"

As the four of us backed to the edge of the tower, I knew this was the voice that spoke when Dana was taken. This was who Argus called the Dark Master. The trickster god—Loki!

"I cannot be ssstopped!" the dark figure cried as

Fenrir pawed the tower stones, flames dripping from his jaws. "Centuries consssspire to begin this war! Argusss, rise! Myrmidons, attack!"

Argus bolted up and came at us, giant arms snatching, bloodshot eyes filled with rage. At the same time, we heard the Myrmidons thundering up the stairs.

Thud! Thud! THUD!

My mind was a mess, but my fingers knew just what to do. Twanging the deepest string, I commanded the circular stairs below us to collapse. The army of Myrmidons climbing the staircase crashed to the floor in a heap, bringing the top of the tower down with them. Argus stumbled to his knees.

I plucked the strings over and over, and the tower itself shook.

"No!" shouted Loki, dragging Fenrir to the edge of the parapet. "The battle has only begun! You sssshall not ssssurvive!" He raised an icy hand to the distance. An explosion rocked the dark sky, and something from the ground shot upward. With a swirl of fog and a cry of rage, Loki and Fenrir leaped from the tower and vanished into smoke below.

"Look!" Dana yelled. Her eyes were fixed on the far distance. "Owen!"

The dark air cleared for a moment, and we could see beyond the tower walls. There was a faraway land of ice-capped volcanoes and whirling snow. Past that were deserts piled with carved white monuments. Beyond that, a land of hanging gardens and palaces of blue and amber stone.

My heart froze.

The Underworlds.

But there was no time to waste. I twanged the highest string of the lyre. The stairs came coiling back up to the roof, and the four of us raced down, tore through the battered doors, and clambered over the mud-ball bridge.

The Myrmidons didn't like that. They pulled themselves up and poured from the tower, hurtling their battle-axes hard. *Wump-wump-wump!* The giant blades struck the ground at our heels. We dodged them and kept running. The whole time, I held Dana's arm tight.

The moment we arrived at the arena—*THUNG!*—the final grain of black sand sank into the bottom of the hourglass.

Hades' face was dark and somber. "You've seen him, then. Loki, the evil trickster god of the North. He stirs up no good and sets the Underworlds at war. Nevertheless, as a beast of my word, I shall honor my bargain. You may take Dana Runson back with you."

I sighed. "Yes!"

"But the game has changed," said Hades. "Loki has shattered the rules. This girl should not have been stolen. More than that, he is freeing monsters, allowing them into your world. Just now, in fact . . ."

"You can't be serious!" said Jon. "You mean that explosion we saw?"

Hades nodded grimly. "Loki has freed the Cyclopes. No doubt you've heard of them."

Dana squeezed my hand. "Giants," she said. "One big eye each. Angry all the time. I saw them early this morning."

Hades snarled coldly. "Turns out those single eyes are good for something. They helped the giants find their way into your world." He paused. "You must bring them back."

"What? No!" I cried. "This is over. We're taking Dana home. You deal with Loki yourself—"

Hades stood to his full height. "I am mighty and I am just! But I am forbidden to walk in your world. Therefore, a second bargain! A simple one. Return the Cyclopes to my Underworld, and Miss Runson may stay with you. That's my deal. Take it or leave it. Or perhaps I should say, take it or leave *her*."

"How are we supposed to capture a couple of huge monsters?" Sydney asked.

"You'll figure it out," Hades said. "You're smart kids."

"Says who?" Jon asked.

Hades turned his dark eyes on Jon. "Oh, you must be the funny one. The comic relief. Well, laugh it up. But, Dana dear, don't forget your toothbrush on your next visit. If you and your friends fail, you will stay longer next time. And speaking of time . . ."

Hades turned the hourglass over, and the grains of black sand began to run down from the top. "I have serious work to do. So get out of my house!"

The hooded figures stood in their seats, pointing their bony fingers back toward the river Styx. "Go! Go! GO!"

Thunder boomed. Lightning crashed. We ran from the arena and didn't stop until we reached the riverbank. A few hazy shapes vanished the instant we got there. Charon's withered face popped up from the reeds.

"You made it!" he said with a wet laugh. "The ghosts were betting against you, but I won. Come on, then. Nearly quitting time."

We piled onto the raft, and the black water swelled beneath its planks. When we docked on the far side of the river, Charon tipped his hat. "Shall I keep a tab for you?" he asked.

"Excuse me?" said Dana.

"I reckon you'll be back," said Charon.

I knew he was right. We would be back.

As we made our way through the scorched rocks, I couldn't stop thinking about what we'd seen from the top of the tower. The Underworlds. Could we possibly come through on this bargain? Could we capture some angry, one-eyed giants? Could we find a way to . . . survive?

Finally, we found the entrance to the boiler room. A minute later, we were in the school basement, and the boiler room door was just a door.

Looking down the hallways, it seemed like forever since we'd been there. It must have felt even longer for Dana. I helped her up the stairs and through the halls to the front of the school. Breathless and afraid, we walked out under the dusky sky.

I paused. "Dana? Can you tell us what it was like?"

She shut her eyes, then opened them. "Dark. Hopeless. Sad. It's what we saw from the tower. Some places are hot, some freezing. Deserts. Snowstorms. All the different Underworlds. Monsters are gathering everywhere. Norse, Egyptian, Greek. All of them. And Loki's behind it."

I looked into her eyes. "But why you? Why did he take you?"

"Something I know?" she said. "Something I saw? My parents suspected that Loki wasn't just a myth. That he was . . . active. I heard them talking. They went to Iceland to find out more. Maybe Loki thinks I know something, too."

"Maybe you do," said Sydney simply.

Dana gazed into the pinewoods behind school. "I should leave here. Hide. Find my parents and leave you all out of this."

My heart pounded inside my chest like a drum in a heavy metal band. I took Dana's arm. "No," I said. "We're already in it. And we'll do what we need to do to keep you here."

Lightning flashed suddenly over the school, and the first cold raindrops fell. Sydney checked her cell. It was dinnertime.

"First thing in the morning, we find out where the Cyclopes are playing house," said Jon. "Then we boot them back below."

I only hoped it would be as simple as that.

But when I breathed in long and slow to calm myself, I smelled smoke.

The battle *was* beginning. It was dark. It was dangerous. It was deadly.

And we were right in the middle of it.

RIVER STYX

ARENA

HADES'
THRONE

GREEK

NORSE

EGYPTIAN

BABYLONIAN

GLOSSARY

Argus (Greek Mythology): a beast with 100 eyes

Cerberus (Greek Mythology): a three-headed dog; prevents the dead from leaving the Underworld

Charon (Greek Mythology): a ferryman who leads the souls of the dead across the river Styx to the Underworld

Cyclopes (Greek Mythology): one-eyed giants

Fenrir (Norse Mythology): a giant, fire-breathing red wolf

Hades (Greek Mythology): the ruler of the Underworld

Jason (Greek Mythology): a human hero of many adventures

ARGUS

CERBERUS

FENRIR

Loki (Norse Mythology): a trickster god

Lyre of Orpheus (Greek mythology): a stringed instrument that charms people, animals, and objects into doing things for Orpheus

Myrmidons (Greek Mythology): skilled warriors

Odin (Norse Mythology): the chief Norse god

Orpheus (Greek Mythology): a musician who had traveled to the Underworld to bring his wife back from the dead—but didn't succeed

River Styx (Greek Mythology): a river that divides the land of the living from the land of the dead

Valkyries (Norse Mythology): women who work for Odin; choose who lives and dies in battle

LYRE OF ORPHEUS   MYRMIDON   VALKYRIE

THE ADVENTURE IS JUST BEGINNING!

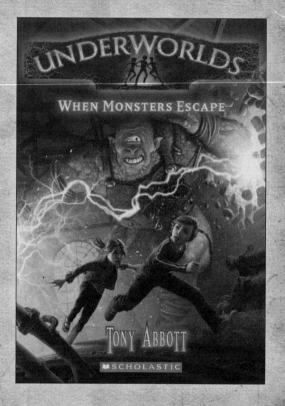

FIND OUT WHAT OWEN, JON, SYDNEY, AND DANA ARE UP AGAINST NEXT. . . .

MY NAME IS OWEN BROWN, AND MY FOREHEAD FEELS like it's an anvil that someone keeps pounding with a red-hot hammer.

Also my teeth hurt, my eyes sting, and my fingers ache.

But ever since my friends and I rescued Dana Runson from the Greek Underworld three days ago, pain has been the new normal—

"Owen, move it!"

I glanced across the wet school parking lot. Dana was racing toward me. Jon Doyle and Sydney Lamberti were right on her heels.

"Out of the way, O—" Jon yelled.

All three of them tackled me and rolled me to the side as —*whoom!*—a small car smashed down from above, landed on the sidewalk, and skittered past us, sparking like crazy.

Just beyond it was a giant, all muscles, all shaggy hair . . . and all one huge eye. He was a Cyclops, one of two Greek monsters who escaped into our world. He was ugly, and he was mad.

Crash! An uprooted flagpole slammed down on the car and bent in half. The second giant had thrown that. He was just as ugly, just as mad, and just as one-eyed. But he had no hair at all.

"Uh, thank—" I said.

"Just run!" Dana screamed, yanking me to my feet and tugging me around the side of the school.